Lola and the Rent-a-Cat
© 2007 – Baeckens Books, Mechelen, Belgium.
Originally published by Zirkoon, Amsterdam, Holland.
© Text and illustrations: Ceseli Josephus Jitta
Lay out: Renée Koldewijn
Produced by Creations for Children International, Belgium
www.c4ci.com
This edition first published in Great Britain and in the USA in 2010
by Frances Lincoln Children's Books
4 Torriano Mews, Torriano Avenue, London NW5 2RZ

www.franceslincoln.com

A catalogue record for this book is available from the British Library.

ISBN: 978-1-84780-139-5

Printed in Quarry Bay, Hong Kong, China, by Sun Fung Offset Printing
in January 2010

1 2 3 4 5 6 7 8 9

Lola and the Rent-a-Cat

Ceseli Josephus Jitta

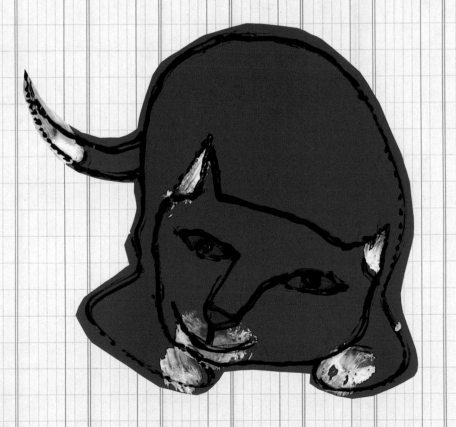

Lola and John have been married since they were young.

Together they can reach anywhere and together they stay balanced.

Together they look after each other and together they remember the shopping list.

Lola and John grow old together.

Sometimes John is sad for no reason
and loses his way around the house.

It's hard for him to get down stairs,
and that makes Lola sad, too.

One day John falls over.
His heart stops beating.

The funeral is tomorrow. Lola closes the curtains for John for the very last time.

After fifty-six years, she is alone again.

The days are long.
There is no one
to look after any more.
She reads, she watches TV
and she surfs the internet.

One night she visits www.rentacat.com

Experienced cats offer you
company and affection
in return for board
and lodging for any length
of time.

She takes a look at all the cats, and then another look at some of them.

26 GUS
- Stays inside
- Sits on lap
- Eats fresh fish

108 PETE
- Well behaved
- Reliable
- Eats anything

97 FRED
- Out at night
- Loves parties
- Eats fresh meat

258 UDO
- Balcony cat
- Very calm
- Eats dry food

But number 313 is her favourite.

313 TIM

- *Homely, slightly older cat*
- *Loves attention and care*
- *Fond of diet food*

- **Click here to order**

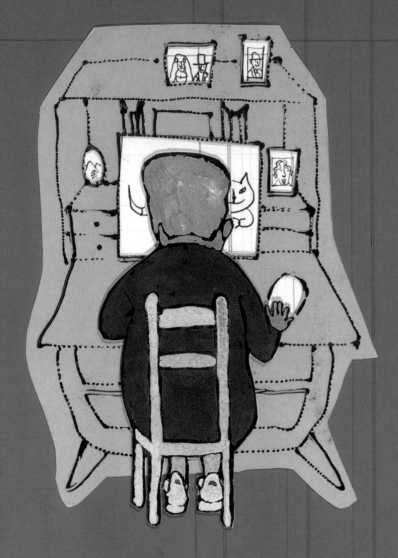

A cat is cosy.
You can love a cat.
Lola's heart beats faster.
She takes a deep breath and fills in the form:

lola.fink@hotmail.com wants to order Tim, number 313

She clicks the 'send' button.
In the blink of an eye the reply appears:

Tim will be with you tomorrow morning.

Yours sincerely,
www.rentacat.com

That night Lola can't sleep. She gets up very early.

Tim!

They are together . . .

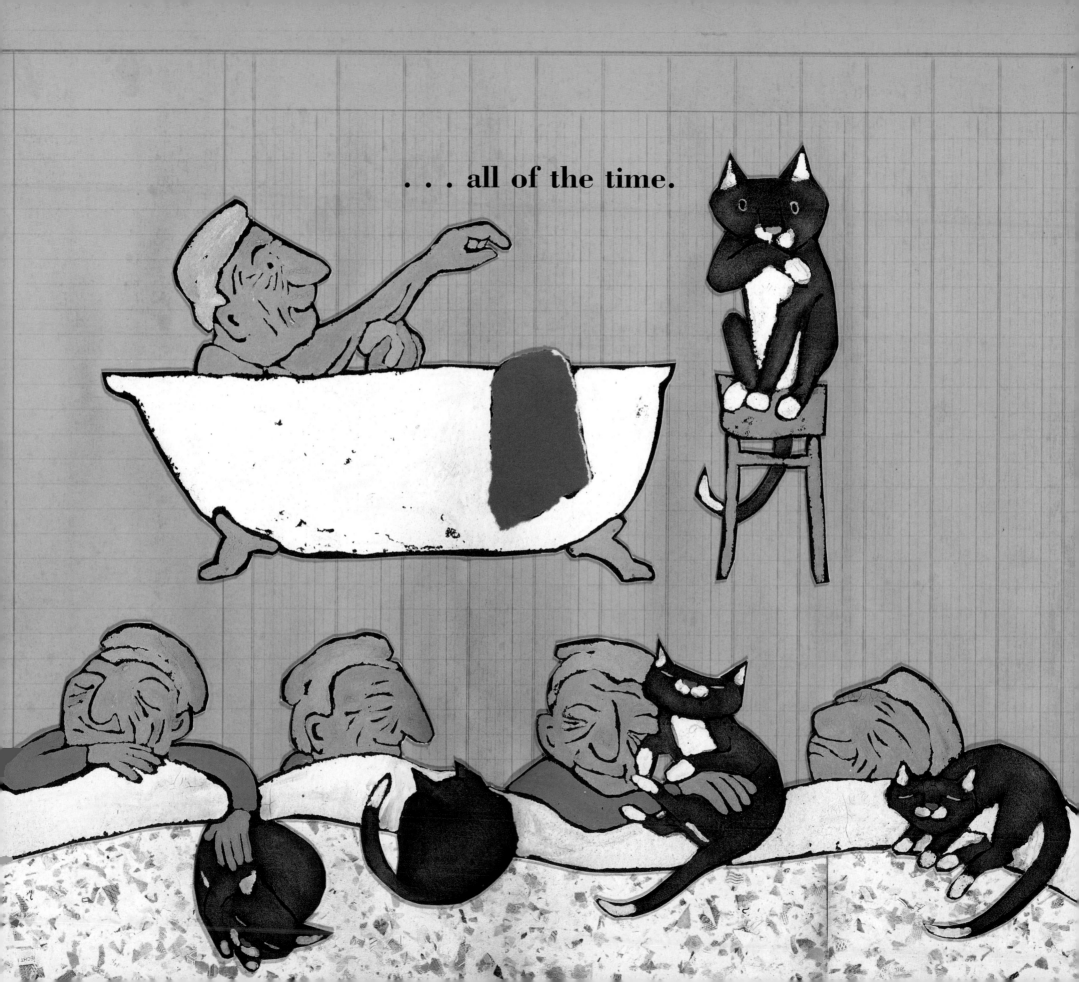

And time flies when you're having fun.

At night they sit together
on the bench in front of
the house.
Tim purrs.
Lola strokes Tim.
She thinks about
the old days.

About the kitten she got for her sixth birthday.

About the afternoons
at the cinema
with her best friend.

About how she fell in love with her husband John . . .

. . . and he with her.

And about the long summer evenings together on the bench in front of the house.

Her tea is getting cold. Lola gets to her feet.
'Off to bed, Tim. Tomorrow is another day.'